This book belongs to

_____

D1307221

Published by Lima Bear Press, LLC
PO Box 354, Montchanin, DE 19710-0354
BULK ORDERS: bulkorders@limabearpress.com

Visit us on the web at
www.limabearpress.com

Printed in China

Copyright © 2008 by Charles A. Neebe.
All rights reserved.

This book may not be reproduced in whole or in part, by any means (with the exception of short quotes
for the purpose of review), without permission of the publisher. For information regarding
permission(s), write to: Lima Bear Press, PO Box 354, Montchanin, DE 19710-0354

Book & Cover design by: George Clements and rosa+wesley, inc.

FIRST EDITION
ISBN: 978-1-933872-25-4

Library of Congress Control Number: 2008920449

THE UMA BEAR STORIES

THE Treasure Hunt

STORY BY

Charles A. Neebe

ILLUSTRATIONS BY

Len DiSalvo

LIMA BEAR PRESS, LLC

The map

It began one morning when Lima Bear found an old bottle washed up by the edge of the cove behind his house. The cork had loosened, and he was able to pull it out. Inside the bottle, Lima Bear saw a folded paper. He was curious, so he crawled in, climbed around behind the folded paper, and pushed it out.

This was easy for him, because Lima Bear was no ordinary bear. He was a special kind of very small bear, only about the size of a lima bean. In fact, Lima Bear looked very much like a lima bean—a lima bean with green fur and tiny arms and legs, that is.

Lima Bear unfolded the paper and saw that it was a treasure map! It showed an 'X' marking the location of a treasure buried on an island far across the sea.

"How wonderful!" Lima Bear thought. He had always wanted to find a treasure. He rushed out to tell his friends. He found Maskamal the raccoon and Whistle-Toe the rabbit and Fresna the otter. They agreed it was a genuine treasure map, and they all wanted to go on the treasure hunt.

"We'll be rich, we'll be rich," Maskamal sang as they danced around the map.

The first thing they would need, Whistle-Toe pointed out, was a big ship—one big enough to sail an ocean, big enough for stormy seas, big enough to scare off sea monsters, big enough to carry treasure, and big enough to flee from pirates.

It was a spirit-dampening thought. "How will we ever find a ship like that?" Lima Bear sighed.

"We'll need a lot of money," Fresna said.

Things did not look promising.

Suddenly Whistle-Toe said, "I've got it!"

"The money?" Lima Bear asked.

"No, no, not the money," Whistle-Toe said. "How to get the money. We'll have a fund-raiser."

"What's that?" Maskamal asked.

"Never heard of such a thing," Fresna said.

"How does it work?" Lima Bear asked.

"Simple," Whistle-Toe said. "We each contribute all our money to the fund. Then maybe we'll have enough for a big ship."

They all went home and brought back their money.

"Let's start with you, Maskamal," Whistle-Toe said. "You're the biggest, so you probably have the most."

But Maskamal was not good at saving money. In fact, he was a lot better at spending it.

"Hmmmmm," Maskamal said, rubbing his chin. "Maybe we should start with the smallest one first." He looked over toward Lima Bear.

"Come on, Maskamal," Fresna said. "Show us how much you brought."

"Well, all right." Maskamal cleared his throat. "I brought these." He held out a coupon and a note and set them on the ground in front of his friends.

"Those don't look like money," Lima Bear said. "What are they, exactly?"

"This one is a coupon," Maskamal said. "For 15-cents off."

"15-cents off what?" Fresna asked.

"I'm not sure," Maskamal said. Maskamal could only read numbers and a few letters, not words.

But Whistle-Toe could read. He picked up the coupon and looked at it. "It says: '15-cents off for Quiggily-Wiggily's Toothpaste'."

"There," Maskamal said. "That's what it's for."

"But what good is it?" Whistle-Toe asked.

"Everybody needs toothpaste," Maskamal said. "We can sell the coupon."

"I don't think this fund-raiser is starting off so well," Lima Bear said.

Whistle-Toe put down the coupon. "What's the other thing?"

"Oh, this? I think that's an IOU for 40 cents," Maskamal said. "We can collect it and put the money in the fund."

Whistle-Toe read the note. "Maskamal, this is my IOU. It says you owe me 40 cents. How did you get this, anyway?"

"I found it on the path," Maskamal said.

"Yes, I remember now," Whistle-Toe said. "You do owe me 40 cents. I'd forgotten all about it. Why didn't you give this back to me when you found it?"

"I didn't know it was yours. I could only read the '40'. I can't read words. You know that."

"I'm going to keep this," Whistle-Toe said. "And this time I won't lose it."

"Well, I guess then maybe you should put the 40 cents in the fund for me," Maskamal said.

"Wait a minute, Maskamal," Whistle-Toe said. "If I do that, aren't you putting my money into the fund?"

"It's all I have," Maskamal said.

"I think we need to move on," Lima Bear said.

"You're right," Whistle-Toe said. "We'll go to the smallest one next to see if we can get this fund-raiser off to a better start. Lima Bear?"

Lima Bear had never earned any money, because he was too little. The only money he had was money he had found. Once he came across a half-dollar in the woods, but it was too heavy for him to carry alone, and by the time he found some friends to help him with it, someone else had already picked it up. Another time, though, he tripped over a dime on the trail and he was able to roll it back to his house all by himself. The dime was his life's savings. He put it in the fund.

"Well," Whistle-Toe said, looking at the dime and trying to hide his disappointment, "it looks like we have made a beginning."

"At least it's money," Fresna said.

With contributions now in from two of them, they were at the half-way point. So far they had a dime and a 15-cents off coupon for toothpaste, and their prospects of buying a big ship looked dim indeed. Things picked up a little with Whistle-Toe's turn. He contributed his savings of two quarters and seven pennies, bringing the fund total to 67 cents.

All their hopes now hinged on Fresna, the last contributor. She opened up her wallet and, to their amazement, started counting out dollar bills: one, two, three, four, five—all the way up to nineteen. Nineteen dollars! The others had never seen so much money in their lives. Maskamal stared wide-eyed at the pile of bills, thinking of all the things he could buy with it.

The fund-raiser was a success. The fund had almost twenty dollars, more than enough, they were sure, to buy a big ship. Lima Bear, Whistle-Toe and Maskamal were overjoyed, certain now that they really would be going on a treasure hunt.

But Fresna did not seem to be as happy as the others.

"What's the matter, Fresna?" Lima Bear asked.

"I don't know," Fresna said.

"Come on, you can tell us," Lima Bear said.

"It's just . . . . it's just that the fund is almost all my money. That isn't fair, is it?"

"We all put in everything we had," Whistle-Toe said. "That's fair, isn't it?"

"I certainly put in everything I had," Maskamal said.

"I know," Fresna said, "but somehow it's still not fair."

"Fresna is right," Lima Bear said. "After all, without her, the fund-raiser would not have been a success."

"I would have put in just as much if I'd had it," Maskamal said.

"Still," Lima Bear said, "it's only fair that we do something special for Fresna. I know." He turned to Fresna. "You can be the Captain."

"Captain of the ship?" Fresna asked.

"Yes," Lima Bear said. "You'll steer the ship and give the orders, and we'll do the work."

"I would like to be Captain," Fresna said. "That would make it fairer, I guess."

"You can be Captain, then," Whistle-Toe said. "Everyone agreed?" They all nodded.

"I'm glad that's settled," Lima Bear said.

Now they were ready to buy a ship for the treasure hunt. First, though, Whistle-Toe said, they needed to make a copy of the treasure map, just in case they lost the original one. He found a big piece of paper and a small pencil.

"Here, Lima Bear," Whistle-Toe said, handing the pencil to him. "You should have the honor, since you're the one who found the treasure map."

"Don't you think someone else should draw it?" Lima Bear asked.

"No, no," the others said. "You should be the one."

Lima Bear picked up the pencil. Even though it was a short pencil, it was very big for Lima Bear. In fact, when he held it upright, it was taller than he was. He wrapped his arms around the pencil, holding it upright, and started drawing. It was slow work. Every few seconds he had to stop, put the pencil down and look back to the original map to see how it was drawn.

Even so, he kept getting confused. He was so close to the paper that he really couldn't tell where he was on the map or which way he was going. It was like trying to draw by pushing around a big long pole with a pencil tip at the end of it. By the time he was finished, he was huffing and puffing.

"Whew," he said, letting the pencil fall over with a tiny thud. "My arms are out of breath."

The others looked at Lima Bear's map. They looked at the original treasure map. Then they looked at Lima Bear's map again.

Whistle-Toe scratched his head. "It's not quite right, is it?"

Actually, the copy didn't look much like the original. To tell the truth, it didn't look much like anything.

"Shouldn't the 'X' for the treasure go over here?" Whistle-Toe drew an 'X' in a different place from where Lima Bear had drawn it.

"I don't think so," Maskamal said. "I know what the problem is. It's drawn up-side-down." He turned the map around. It didn't look worse that way, but then again it didn't look better either. "There, this is the way it goes, isn't it?" Maskamal drew another 'X' on the map in yet a different place.

"No, that's not it," Fresna said. She turned the map sideways. "I like it better that way."

"You do?" Whistle-Toe said.

"Sure," Fresna said. "Can't you see it? The treasure is over here." She put a fourth 'X' on the map in a different place from the other three.

With four 'X's' on it in four different places, Lima Bear's copy of the treasure map had become very confusing.

"What do you think, Lima Bear?" Whistle-Toe asked. "After all, it's your map."

"I'm not sure," Lima Bear said. "I can't tell which way is right side up any more. I guess it looks okay, though."

"With four 'X's'?" Whistle-Toe asked.

"Maybe there are really four treasures on the island," Maskamal said. His eyes lit up at the thought.

"But we drew the extra 'X's' on the map!" Whistle-Toe said.

"That's right," Lima Bear said. "They weren't on the map we found."

"At least they're on your map," Maskamal said hopefully.

Whistle-Toe shook his head. "That doesn't help us any. This copy really isn't much good. Maybe we should throw it out."

"Oh, no," Lima Bear said. "We should keep it. It's the first map I've ever drawn."

"I like the copy better anyway," Maskamal said. He liked the idea of finding four treasures. "I'll be right back."

Maskamal ran off somewhere and the others started talking about what exactly you do to buy a ship. None of them really knew; the only one who had an idea was Whistle-Toe, who said they had to get a Certificate of Sale when they bought it to prove the ship was theirs. Just then, Maskamal returned, wearing a jacket and tie. Neither one fit well, and he looked silly.

"Why are you wearing that?" Whistle-Toe asked.

"I need to look like a businessman," Maskamal said, "because I'm going to buy us a ship."

"You are?" Fresna asked, worried.

"Yes." Maskamal put Lima Bear's copy and the money in his jacket pocket. Then he picked up the original map and carefully folded it. "There," he said. "For safe keeping. We wouldn't want to lose them."

"No, we certainly wouldn't want to do that," Fresna said.

Lima Bear was still puzzling about how to buy a ship. Then he had an idea. "I know," he said. "My cousin, L. Joe Bean, is very clever. He knows about buying things."

They all agreed that L. Joe Bean should come along and help out. Maskamal said he knew where L. Joe Bean lived, on the other side of the woods, and would stop by for him.

"What about the money and the map?" Whistle-Toe asked.

"They're safe and sound," Maskamal said, putting them inside his jacket pocket.

"Wouldn't it be better to leave those here?" Fresna asked, thinking about what was, after all, mostly her money.

"This is the safest place for them," Maskamal said. "The pocket is very deep and look, I have it buttoned closed."

"Maybe one of us should go with you," Lima Bear said.

"Don't worry, I'll be right back," Maskamal said, and he scampered off before they could say anything. As they watched him disappear into the woods, the others had the uneasy feeling that they should not have let Maskamal go off by himself with all of their valuables.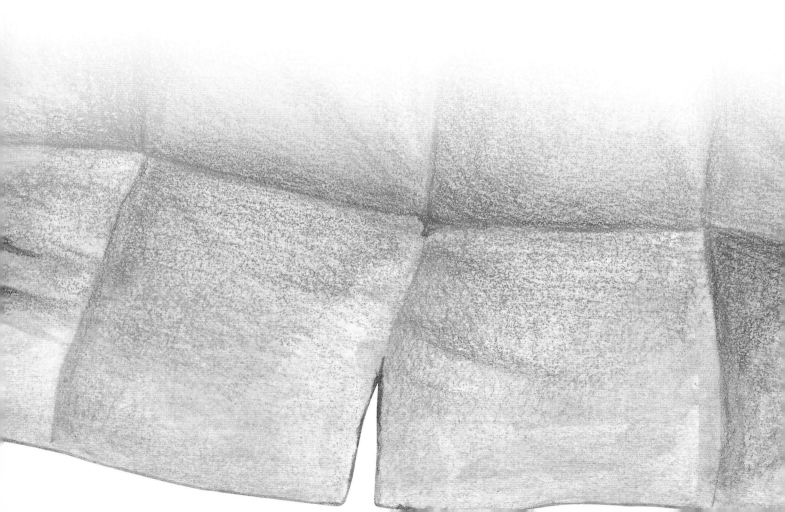

The ship

It was a long way to L. Joe Bean's house, so Maskamal had time to think as he trotted along the path. He thought about what he would buy with his share of the treasure. He thought about how nice it would be if there really were four treasures, and not just one. He also thought about how much he wanted to be Captain of the ship. He pictured himself standing at the wheel, steering the ship and giving orders.

But they had all agreed that Fresna would be Captain. There was no way to change that. Fresna had contributed most of the money to the fund-raiser. That was something special. What could Maskamal do that was special? There didn't seem to be anything. Unless . . . unless, maybe, if he found a beautiful ship all by himself. That would be special. That would surprise them. They would want him to be Captain then. Even Fresna. After all, it would be his ship, the one he found. Maskamal clapped his hands. What a great idea! It would be scary, buying a big ship all by himself, but he would have L. Joe Bean along, and everyone knew that L. Joe Bean was very clever.

L. Joe Bean was near his house swinging in a little hammock he had made out of thread and a patch of cloth as Maskamal came rushing up. Now L. Joe Bean was the size and shape and the deep red color of a kidney bean, but with tiny arms and legs. Unlike Lima Bear, L. Joe Bean had no fur and this was a problem, you see, because without fur he looked just like the kind of bean you eat. Many of his cousins had, in fact, already ended up in bean soup or chili con carne. It was only because L. Joe Bean was so clever that he had managed to stay uncooked so far.

Maskamal told L. Joe Bean everything. "I have the map and the money here," he said pointing to his pocket, "and a copy of the map too, just in case we lose the first one. I need your help to buy a big ship."

"Let me see the maps." L. Joe Bean was good at reading maps.

Maskamal carefully unfolded the original treasure map and then the copy.

"This is a copy?" L. Joe Bean asked, pointing to Lima Bear's map.

"Yes," Maskamal said. "Lima Bear made it from the original one."

"But it doesn't look anything like the other," L. Joe Bean said. "I can't even tell which way is right side up. And why does it have so many 'X's'?"

"We think there may be four treasures buried on the island," Maskamal whispered, rubbing his hands together with delight.

L. Joe Bean gave Maskamal a doubtful look. He knew that the copy of the map was of no value. He also knew that Maskamal was going to need a lot of help.

"I've decided to leave the copy here at your house," Maskamal said, "so it will be in a safe place in case the first one gets lost."

After Maskamal put the copy in L. Joe Bean's house, he set out eagerly on the path toward town with L. Joe Bean riding on his shoulder. Little did Maskamal know that two scoundrels lay in wait along the path: Trickman Wolf and Sly Weasel. They soon spied Maskamal skipping toward them.

"Well, well," Trickman said, looking through his spyglass and licking his lips, "what do we have coming down the path?"

He handed the spyglass to Sly, who saw Maskamal and
the bulge in Maskamal's pocket from his money and map.
Sly laughed and said:

"I think I spy a fool with a very handsome pool
　　of money.
And if we play it cool we will make the fool
　　look funny."

"Just so," Trickman said.

The two villains waited until Maskamal approached
and then stepped out onto the path in front of him. "Hail,
good friend," Trickman said, holding up his hand. "Where
do you go?"

"To buy a ship," Maskamal said.

"A ship?" Trickman said. "This is your lucky day.
We sell ships."

Sly bowed gracefully and said:

"Ah, you're a pleasure to cheat, I mean a pleasure
    to meet.
We two swindle and steal, I mean fairly we deal.

"We'll spin you a yarn, I mean we'll do you
    no harm.
For the ship that you need, We've high, er,
    low prices indeed."

Trickman frowned at Sly and kicked him in the shin.
"Just what kind of ship are you seeking?"
"A big ship," Maskamal said. "A big ship to go on a. . ."
"Don't tell them what it's for," L. Joe Bean interrupted.
He was already suspicious of these two characters.
"Who said that?" Trickman looked around, not seeing
L. Joe Bean.
"My friend here," Maskamal said, pointing to L. Joe Bean
standing on his shoulder.
"Your friend?" Trickman said. The two villains eyed
L. Joe Bean.
Sly said:

"You don't mean this puny bean?
With a small head who's all red?"

"Yes and it is L. Joe Bean if you please," L. Joe Bean said,
standing as tall as he could, which was not very tall.
Trickman frowned at L. Joe Bean, figuring they would
have to get rid of this bean somehow before dealing with
Maskamal. Then he smiled at Maskamal. "You must have
a lot of money for a big ship," he said licking his lips.
"We have nineteen dollar bills," Maskamal said proudly.
"Shhh, Maskamal," L. Joe Bean said stomping on
Maskamal's shoulder.

"Ow!" Maskamal said, hunching his shoulder from the pinprick of pain.

"I'll bet you have that money hidden away in a safe place," Trickman said.

"It couldn't be safer. It's right here," Maskamal, said patting his jacket pocket, "along with our treasure map." Trickman Wolf's ears perked up at the jingle of coins as Maskamal patted his pocket.

"Maskamal!" L. Joe Bean exclaimed, stomping on Maskamal's shoulder again.

"Hey, what do you keep doing that for, L. Joe Bean?"

"Because you are saying too much."

"But we are trying to buy a ship," Maskamal said.

"You're not doing it the right way," L. Joe Bean said.

"A treasure map," Trickman said, licking his lips again. "So that is why you need a big ship? A treasure hunt?"

Maskamal nodded.

"This is your lucky day," Trickman said. "We have just the ship for you. Come with us and we'll show it to you."

"By all means," Maskamal said.

"No, thank you," L. Joe Bean said.

"L. Joe Bean," Maskamal said, "what's the matter with you?"

"We do not want to buy a ship from them."

"Why, in heaven's name, not?" Maskamal asked.

"Because I don't trust them."

"Don't trust us?!?" Trickman exclaimed, looking very sad.

"L. Joe Bean didn't mean it that way," Maskamal said, trying to comfort Trickman.

"Yes I did!"

"Oh!" Trickman groaned, clasping his chest. "And to think, we were only trying to help you. And the special sale ends today, too."

"Special sale?" Maskamal asked. "It ends today? Oh, then I must see the ship."

"No," L. Joe Bean said.

"I'm sorry," Trickman said, pretending to be hurt, "but I can't put up with your friend anymore."

"But I want to see the ship," Maskamal pleaded.

"Here," Trickman said. With one hand he picked L. Joe Bean off Maskamal's shoulder and with the other hand he unbuttoned Maskamal's jacket pocket. He dropped L. Joe Bean in and rebuttoned the pocket. It all happened so fast that L. Joe Bean hardly had time to protest.

And once he was inside the pocket, all his shouting and yelling only came through as muffled sounds. His words could not be heard, but he could hear clearly every word Maskamal and the other two said. "There," Trickman said, "if you want to see the ship of a lifetime, then leave that. . . that bean in your pocket."

"But I . . ."

"No buts about it," Trickman said. "After what that bean said, I won't have anything to do with him."

"Well, I . . ."

"Imagine yourself as Captain of this magnificent ship." That was quite easy for Maskamal to do.

"I do want to see my ship, I mean, the ship," Maskamal said, "but . . ."

"Then come with us, Captain, down to the bay." Trickman put his arm around Maskamal's shoulder, ignoring the muffled sounds of protest coming from Maskamal's pocket.

Trickman led Maskamal out onto a small ledge overlooking the deepest part of the bay. The ledge was almost flush with the water. "There it is," Trickman said gesturing out toward the bay with his hand. Sly nodded and smiled.

Maskamal looked out over the bay but he could not see anything. Anything, that is, except water and Nana-Ka-Poop Island in the distance. "Where's the ship?"

"Right in front of us," Trickman said.

Maskamal stared as hard as he could. "How come I can't see it?"

"Camouflage," Trickman said with a smile.

"Camouflage? What's that?"

"Camouflage," Trickman said, "means hiding something so you can't see it, even when it's right in front of you."

"You mean there really is a ship in front of me?"

"Absolutely," Trickman said. "You're looking right at it."

"That's amazing," Maskamal said. "Is it a big ship?"

"Three masts," Trickman said. "Big enough to sail an ocean."

Maskamal shook his head in wonderment. "A three-master. And I can't even see it. That's what camouflage does?"

"Yep," Trickman said proudly.

"Can you take the camouflage off so I can see it?"

Trickman turned to Sly. "What do you think?" Sly peered all around to make sure no one was watching. Then he nodded yes. "All right," Trickman said. "Here, put this on." He gave Maskamal an old swim mask with its strap missing. "Hold this against your eyes. Now look into the water. You'll see where the ship is hidden."

Maskamal leaned over the ledge and peered into the deep water. Sure enough, just off shore there was a three-masted ship resting on the bottom. It had a big hole on the side and one of the masts had half rotted away. Maskamal pulled his head back out of the water and removed the mask. "It's a big ship all right, but what's it doing on the bottom?"

"This is the great Yola-reena Treasure Ship, and that's where we're hiding it," Trickman explained. "You don't think we would leave a ship like that afloat where anyone could steal it, do you? The best ships are on the bottom of the ocean, you know."

"I thought that was because they had sunk," Maskamal said.

"Well, maybe that's true for some of them," Trickman said, "but most of them are down there for safekeeping. Like this one."

Muffled sounds came from Maskamal's jacket pocket as L. Joe Bean was shouting at the top of his voice, trying to warn Maskamal.

"It looks kind of rotten," Maskamal said.

"Camouflage," Trickman winked.

"That's camouflage, too?" Maskamal was amazed.

"Yep," Trickman said. "It fools everybody,"

"Boy, it could have fooled me," Maskamal said. "It looks like an old rotten ship."

Trickman beamed proudly. "It took a long time to make it look like that." There were more muffled sounds from Maskamal's jacket pocket. "And it can be all yours. On sale. Right, Sly?"

Sly danced a jig, singing:

"It's a whale of a sale.
    You can sail through a gale.
In the rain or the hail.
    And there's no need to bail.
With a bucket or a pail.
    And if that's just a tale.
You can put us both in jail."

Trickman scowled at Sly for that last comment and kicked him hard in the shin.

"I'd like to buy it," Maskamal said eagerly. "How much is it?" The muffled sounds from Maskamal's jacket pocket sounded more frantic now.

"It's on sale, today only," Trickman said. "Half price."

"Half price!" Maskamal exclaimed.

"It's your lucky day." Trickman said.

"It certainly is. How much is it?"

"I have to figure it out," Trickman said. "Let's see," he said, rubbing his chin, "how much did you say you have in your pocket?"

"I have nineteen dollar bills," Maskamal said.

"I thought I heard some coins in your pocket too," Trickman said, not one to miss any opportunity.

"I almost forgot. I also have 67 cents."

"Is that everything?" Trickman asked, raising his eyebrows.

"Not quite," Maskamal said. "I also have a 15-cents off coupon."

"What?"

"15-cents off for Quiggily-Wiggily's Toothpaste."

"I see," Trickman said. "All right, let me calculate the sale price."

He took out a pencil and paper and began writing. Maskamal hoped he would have enough money for the ship, and paid no attention to the muffled sounds that kept coming from his jacket pocket. Trickman shook his head slowly and wrote down more numbers. Maskamal was mighty worried.

At last Trickman put down his pencil and held up the piece of paper. "Can you believe that?" he said. Sly looked over Trickman's shoulder and shook his head in amazement. "Look at this, my friend," Trickman said to Maskamal. "The sale price comes to $19.67, exactly what you have, to the penny! Amazing."

Maskamal breathed a sigh of relief. "I guess this really is my lucky day."

"It surely is," Trickman said. "Now if you'll just give me your money, the Yola-reena is yours."

"Gladly," Maskamal said, dreaming about how surprised the others would be to see the magnificent ship he had bought and about how they would surely want to make him Captain. Maskamal unbuttoned his jacket pocket for the money. A glimmer of light greeted L. Joe Bean, taking him out of the darkness he had been in since being buttoned up inside the pocket. He was sputtering mad at Maskamal.

"Don't do it, Maskamal," he yelled. "Don't you see what they're up to?" He tried to grab hold of one of the dollar bills as Maskamal pulled the money out, but he slipped off and fell back to the bottom of the pocket.

"Maskamal," he called out, scrambling back to his feet, "they're cheating... " Just then it became dark again as Trickman buttoned Maskamal's pocket closed.

"Careful," Trickman said. "You don't want to lose your treasure map."

L. Joe Bean's warnings hadn't awakened Maskamal from his dreaming, but they did make him remember what Whistle-Toe had said about a Certificate of Sale. When Trickman held out his hand for the money, Maskamal asked him about the Certificate.

"Certificate?" Trickman asked nervously. "What kind of Certificate?"

"A Certificate of Sale, showing the ship is mine," Maskamal said. "I need to bring it back with me."

"Oh, I see," Trickman said, giving Sly a worried look. "Well, I'm not sure we have it with us."

"You don't have one?" Maskamal said.

"Of course we do," Trickman said. "It's just . . . do you need to read it?"

"No." Maskamal shuffled his feet, feeling a little embarrassed. "You see, I can't read. I just have to bring it back with me."

"Oh," Trickman said, brightening. "Maybe we have it with us after all. Sly, do you have that Certificate?"

Sly thought for a moment and then his eyes lit up and he pulled out a paper from his back pocket and handed it to Maskamal, singing:

"Ah, we have what you need.
  A Certificate indeed.
We beg you, we plead
  don't suspect a misdeed."

That last line earned Sly another kick from Trickman.

"So this is the Certificate." Maskamal was pleased that he remembered to ask for it.

"That's it all right." Trickman held out his hand again, and Maskamal gave him the money.

Maskamal examined the Certificate curiously. "What's this in the center?"

"That?" Trickman said, clearing his throat. "Why that's the . . . that's the captain's wheel. You know, for steering the Yola-reena."

"Funny," Maskamal laughed, "it looks like a picture of a pie."

"Yes, it does," Trickman laughed. "How odd."

"Can you read me what the Certificate says?" Maskamal asked.

"By all means." Trickman put his arm around Maskamal's shoulder. "It says: 'This is to certify that . . .' What did you say your name was again?"

"Maskamal."

"Oh yes, of course." He began again. "This is to certify that Maskamal, Maskamal the Captain, has purchased the Yola-reena to sail the seas in search of. . . ."

Trickman continued reciting the Certificate. As he did so, Sly sneaked up next to Maskamal and, with a small pair of scissors, cut out a big section of Maskamal's jacket at the bottom, just under the pocket. Maskamal was too spellbound by Trickman's words to feel anything.

With L. Joe Bean it was a different story. As the scissors cut into the bottom of the pocket they nearly sliced him in two. He leaped to escape the sharp blades and fell out of the gaping hole in the bottom of the pocket, hitting the ground so hard he was winded. Sly did not see him fall out.

The treasure map fell out as well, and so did the Quiggily-Wiggily's Toothpaste coupon. Sly scooped up the map and stepped on the coupon, covering it with his foot. Fortunately he missed L. Joe Bean.

Trickman finished "reading" the Certificate and gave it back to Maskamal, who proceeded to unbutton his jacket pocket and drop the Certificate in. Maskamal was a little surprised, and also pleased, not to hear L. Joe Bean shouting again as he unbuttoned his pocket. "At last he's stopped," Maskamal thought.

Naturally the Certificate fell right out as soon as it was put in. Quick as a wink, Sly put his other foot over it so Maskamal wouldn't see it.

Maskamal bid farewell to Trickman and Sly and hurried off to tell his friends the good news. He was so excited he forgot all about L. Joe Bean, who as far as he knew, was still buttoned up inside his pocket. He skipped along happily. Surely the others would want to make him Captain now.

The switch

As soon as Maskamal was out of sight, Trickman and Sly burst into laughter and shook hands. They opened up the treasure map and looked at it with delight. Meanwhile, L. Joe Bean had recovered from his terrible fall.

He had to warn the others before these two scoundrels disappeared with all their money and the map. It would take him a long time with his tiny legs to get back to the others. He had to hurry. But just as he started to scurry away, Trickman saw L. Joe Bean and scooped him up.

"What have we here," Trickman said. "A pesky little bean, I see. You seem to like pockets so you can try this one for a while." He plopped L. Joe Bean into his pocket. There he stayed until the two scoundrels returned to their hideout, at which time Trickman took him out and handed him over to Sly, saying, "Here, tie him up."

Sly looked at Trickman.

"Wolf, I'll gladly do your bidding
    But to tie him up? You're kidding!
  You can't tie up a bean
    You must see what I mean."

Sly was right of course. There was no way to tie up L. Joe Bean.

"What then?" Trickman asked.

Sly licked his chops as he sang.

"Beans are something to eat,
    they're a real fine treat.
  In some sauce and some meat,
    It's a meal you can't beat."

"Good idea," and with that Trickman tossed L. Joe Bean into a pot of stew that was heating up on the fire. L. Joe Bean landed on a big piece of potato. Poor L. Joe Bean. It looked as if he was going to now suffer the same fate as had many of his cousins. The stew was heating up mighty fast. He would have to think quickly to get out uncooked. The piece of potato was already very warm.

"What's that I hear?" Trickman said suddenly. "Laughter?" Sly cocked his ear:

"Aye, there's a sound in the air.
　　Let us look with great care
That we may know from where
　　comes this laughter so fair."

They followed the sound to the fire and sure enough, it was coming from the pot of stew. L. Joe Bean was laughing as loud as he could.

"What are you laughing for, Bean?" Trickman asked. "You're being cooked. That's no reason to laugh."

"I know, I know," L. Joe Bean laughed, "but I can't help it. I keep thinking of you two trying to find the treasure with that map."

"What's so funny about that?" Trickman asked.

"It's not the real map." L. Joe Bean laughed even louder. "We have the real map and what's more there are . . ." He couldn't finish, he was laughing so hard. The potato was almost too hot to stand on now.

"There are what?" Trickman asked.

"There are four treasures on the real map," L. Joe Bean said slapping his knee with laughter.

"Wait a minute." Trickman plucked up L. Joe Bean just as his feet were about to sizzle. "You get out of that pot and tell us what's going on here."

"We made a fake map," L. Joe Bean said, still hardly able to control his laughter. "You don't think we would let someone like Maskamal walk around with the real map, do you?"

"Hmmm." Trickman thought about that for a minute. "You know, Sly, the Bean may be right. No one would ever let a fool walk around with a real treasure map. Now, it is we who have been fooled." He turned back to L. Joe Bean. "You said four treasures?"

"Four big treasures," L. Joe Bean said.

"And just where is this map?" Trickman asked, angry for having been fooled by a fake map.

"It's in my secret hiding place," L. Joe Bean said.

"I'll tell you what," Trickman said. "You take us there and give us that map and we will set you free."

"Well, I don't know," L. Joe Bean said, not wanting to look too eager. His feet were beginning to cool off a little. "What about Maskamal's money?"

"What about it?" Trickman grinned. "It's a tidy sum, isn't it?"

"Not much compared to four big treasures full of diamonds and rubies and gold," L. Joe Bean said.

Trickman's and Sly's eyes bulged at the thought of such riches.

"But that small amount of money means a lot to Maskamal," L. Joe Bean continued. "So if you give me back the money and promise to set me free, I'll take you there."

"It's a deal." Trickman put L. Joe Bean on his shoulder and L. Joe Bean led them to his house. Before he would show them the other map, he made them put Maskamal's money down the hollow of a nearby dead tree with a beehive inside. The bees were L. Joe Bean's friends, and he knew that they would sting the two scoundrels if they ever tried to take the money back.

Only after the money was safe and sound did he show Trickman and Sly the other map. Trickman held it up. He and Sly saw the four 'X's' on the map showing where treasures were located. They licked their lips. But there was something strange about the map. Neither one could tell which way was right side up.

Trickman turned the map to the right and thought that it looked better that way. Sly turned it to the left and thought it looked better that way. But they really couldn't be sure one way or the other. Finally Trickman turned to L. Joe Bean.

"Bean, how does this map go, anyway?" he asked.

"It's simple," L. Joe Bean said. "If the right way is the wrong way, then the left way is the right way, because if the left way's not the right way, then the only way that's left is the right way, which is wrong."

"Huh?" Trickman said.

Sly scratched his head, bewildered, and said:

"Now wait a minute, Bean.
 We don't know what you mean.
 You say right, then left, then right.
 You'll next say black is white."

"Here, show us how it goes," Trickman said.

"Turn it counter-clockwise," L. Joe Bean said.

Trickman turned it to the left one turn and studied it. "That's not right," he said.

"You're right," L. Joe Bean said. "It's left. Turn it again."

So Trickman turned the map another turn to the left. "That's not right either," he said.

"Yes, it's left again, isn't it," L. Joe Bean said. "Turn it again."

Trickman turned it one more time and then studied the map. "That can't be it either," he said, shaking his head.

"Try it once more," L. Joe Bean suggested. Trickman turned it a fourth turn. "There, that's it now," L. Joe Bean said.

"But that's how I was holding it in the first place," Trickman said.

"Well, then, you must have been right all along," L. Joe Bean said.

Trickman scratched his head. "This is a very strange map. Are you sure this is the real treasure map?" He looked at L. Joe Bean suspiciously.

"No question about it," L. Joe Bean said. "The real map shows the four treasures."

Trickman was not completely convinced. "Then how come this real one looks so new and the fake one looks so old?"

"Ah," L. Joe Bean said thinking quickly. "That's the camouflage."

"I don't follow," Trickman said.

"We traced the original treasure map to make it look new and then threw the original one away. And then we found an old fake map we could pretend was the real one."

"Hmmm," Trickman said. "I guess that means we can just throw this old fake map away then, doesn't, it?" He watched to see L. Joe Bean's reaction.

"Fine with me." L. Joe Bean shrugged, pretending not to care. L. Joe Bean's coolness convinced Trickman that the map with the four 'X's' was the real one.

"All right," Trickman said to Sly, "let's go get these four treasures with this map. So long, Bean." As they started off, Trickman took out the other map, the old one they had stolen from Maskamal, crinkled it up into a ball and tossed it away.

L. Joe Bean's heart sank as he saw the map land in a small stream. As soon as the two scoundrels were out of sight, he rushed over to chase after the map. It had caught in a snag in the middle of the stream. It was already starting to pull apart in the water.

L. Joe Bean couldn't swim, so he looked around for something to use as a boat. He found half of an old walnut shell at the edge of the water. He pushed the shell into the water and leaped aboard. He drifted right down to the map, but no sooner had the shell touched the map then it capsized, dumping L. Joe Bean into the water.

L. Joe Bean struggled to keep from going under until, at last, he was able to pull himself onto the bank. He was too exhausted to try to reach the map again. As he watched, helpless, the treasure map slowly pulled apart and disappeared. With a heavy heart, L. Joe Bean, started off to find Lima Bear and his other friends.

The treasure

Meanwhile, Maskamal had returned, proud as a peacock. Lima Bear, Whistle-Toe and Fresna listened as he described the magnificent Yola-reena, and how he had had just enough money, to the penny, to buy it.

"Where's L. Joe Bean?" Lima Bear asked.

"Oh, I almost forgot. He's right here." Maskamal unbuttoned his jacket pocket and reached into it. To his great surprise and to the surprise of the others, his hand came right out at the bottom. "What's this?!?" Maskamal exclaimed.

"It's your hand, I think," Lima Bear said, now suddenly concerned about the whereabouts of his cousin.

"Where is L. Joe Bean?" Maskamal cried out, feeling around in his pocket. "Oh, no, everything is gone," he moaned looking into the hole that was once the bottom of his pocket. "The map, the Certificate of Sale, even my coupon."

"How could this have happened?" Fresna cried.

"I don't know," Maskamal said. "My pocket must have gotten torn."

"It looks like it's been cut out," Whistle-Toe said, staring at the neat hole.

"You're right, it does," Maskamal said, puzzled.

"What was L. Joe Bean doing in your pocket, anyway?" Whistle-Toe asked.

"Oh, Trickman put him there because he was interfering," Maskamal said.

"Interfering?" Whistle-Toe asked. "What do you mean, 'interfering'?"

"He wouldn't go see the ship."

"Why not?" Fresna asked.

"Something about him not trusting Trickman and Sly," Maskamal said.

"Hmmmm," Whistle-Toe said. He knew L. Joe Bean was very smart, and it wasn't good news that L. Joe Bean had not trusted the two characters Maskamal had met.

They all agreed the best thing was to try to find L. Joe Bean and hopefully the map and the other things as well. They retraced Maskamal's steps back to the place where he had met Trickman and Sly. Right away they spotted the two pieces of paper still folded up and lying where Sly had stepped on them.

Maskamal picked them up. "We're on the right track. This is my 15 cents-off coupon and here is the Certificate of Sale." He handed the papers to Whistle-Toe.

"Wait a minute," Whistle-Toe said. "This isn't a Certificate of Sale."

"Sure it is," Maskamal said. "You can tell by the Captain's wheel in the center of the paper."

"Captain's wheel!?" Whistle-Toe exclaimed. "That's not a Captain's wheel, it's a picture of an apple pie." He showed the flyer to Lima Bear and Fresna. "All this paper says is: 'Grandpa Zoozo's Apple Pies, Fresh and Nutritious, Always Delicious'. Maskamal, you didn't really think this was your Certificate, did you?"

"Well, er," Maskamal said, his face turning red.

"Didn't L. Joe Bean tell you what it said?" Lima Bear asked. "He knows how to read."

"No," Maskamal said shuffling his feet. "You see, he was in my pocket. But anyway I got a real nice ship for us."

Whistle-Toe and Fresna glanced at each other. If this was the Certificate, they were afraid to imagine what the ship was going to look like.

"Maskamal, are you sure you bought a ship?" Whistle-Toe asked. "A real ship?"

"Yes, I'm sure," Maskamal said. "I saw it with my own eyes."

"It wasn't an apple pie or something, was it?" Fresna asked.

"Of course not," Maskamal said, annoyed. "What do you think I am anyway, a fool?"

Whistle-Toe and Fresna did not reply. Instead they kept looking for L. Joe Bean and the treasure map, but no matter how hard they searched, they could find no sign of either.

Then they remembered that L. Joe Bean would be looking for them, too. L. Joe Bean would go back to the ship Maskamal had bought, thinking that sooner or later, they would all want to see it. They decided to go there and wait for L. Joe Bean, and also to get a look at the ship Maskamal had bought, if it really was a ship.

So off they went, Maskamal leading the way. His spirits rose at the thought of how quickly the others would forget about his 'apple pie' Certificate as soon as they saw the magnificent Yola-reena. He led them out onto the ledge overhanging the bay.

"There it is," he said. The other three stared out at the bay and, of course, they could see nothing. Nothing, that is, except Nana-Ka-Poop Island in the distance.

"Where, exactly?" Whistle-Toe asked uneasily.

"Right in front of you."

"You don't mean Nana-Ka-Poop Island, do you?" Fresna asked in a worried voice.

"Of course not. Don't be silly," Maskamal said.

"Well, I don't see any ship," Fresna said, now more concerned than ever.

"Of course not," Maskamal said. "It's camouflaged."

"What does that mean?" Whistle-Toe asked.

"It means that it's right in front of you but it's hidden so you can't see it."

"Why is it hidden?" Lima Bear asked.

"So no one will steal it," Maskamal said.

"Well, it certainly is hidden," Fresna said. "I can't see a thing."

"Show us where it is," Whistle-Toe said.

"Gladly," Maskamal said. "But I have to show you one at a time." Maskamal picked up the old worn-out swim mask he had used earlier and handed it to Whistle-Toe. "Here, hold this up against your face," he said. "Let Lima Bear get inside first."

Whistle-Toe put Lima Bear inside the mask and pushed it on over his eyes. Maskamal showed him where to look underwater. Whistle-Toe was so dumbfounded by what he saw that he gasped and took in a mouthful of water. He came up sputtering for air, pulling the mask off so fast that poor Lima Bear almost fell out.

"Maskamal!!" He exclaimed. "You didn't!! I don't believe it!"

"What is it??" Fresna said, grabbing the face mask and looking underwater herself. She came up equally dumbfounded. "Oh, no Maskamal, how could you!" she cried. "With all my money!"

"What's the matter?" Maskamal asked, still proud of his purchase.

"Maskamal, you bought a shipwreck," Whistle-Toe said.

"A shipwreck? What do you mean?" Maskamal asked.

"You bought an old rotten ship," Fresna said.

"I didn't think it was rotten," Maskamal said.

"What about the big hole and the broken mast?" Fresna asked.

"That's part of the camouflage," Maskamal said. "That's what they told me."

"Maskamal, Maskamal," Whistle-Toe moaned, shaking his head. "I don't believe it. Not even you could do this."

"You mean it's just a sunken ship?" Maskamal asked.

Fresna nodded sadly. She was crestfallen at having lost all her money for this. "I wish we had never found that treasure map," she cried.

It had been a bad day for the friends. L. Joe Bean was lost. The treasure map was gone. They had lost all their money. And all they had to show for this was a worthless shipwreck.

They all felt terrible, and Maskamal felt the worst. He had let his friends down, and all because he had wanted to be Captain. How would he ever make it up to them?

Just then they spotted L. Joe Bean scampering down the path to the ledge. They all jumped up to greet him. Where had he been? What had he been doing? Panting for breath, L. Joe Bean explained.

Their spirits picked up upon learning that their money was safe and sound in the bee tree near L. Joe Bean's house. Their spirits sagged again, however, upon learning that the real treasure map was forever lost.

"I guess we're no worse off than we were before we found the map," Whistle-Toe sighed.

"And we have a ship now," Lima Bear said, trying to be cheerful.

"What good is that?" Whistle-Toe asked.

"I think we should try to raise it," Lima Bear replied.

"It's just an old wreck," Fresna said.

"Even so, I think we should try to bring it up."

"I suppose it won't hurt to try," Fresna said with a shrug.

They would need a strong rope tied around some part of the ship. Fresna had a rope. She offered to swim down with it. Being an otter, she was the best swimmer. Lima Bear volunteered to help Fresna find the best place to tie the rope. Lima Bear found a few of his lightning bug friends, on-and-off bugs as he called them, who agreed to help.

So Fresna put on the face mask with Lima Bear and ten on-and-off bugs inside, took the rope, and dove down to the sunken wreck. As she swam around the ship, the on-and-off bugs all went on and off at the same time, giving Lima Bear enough light to see clearly. Lima Bear spotted a large timber on the side of the ship where they could fasten the rope. Fresna tied the rope securely.

Once back on shore, they all pulled as hard as they could on the rope. That is, Fresna, Maskamal and Whistle-Toe pulled on the rope. Lima Bear

and L. Joe Bean weren't big enough to get their hands around the rope, so instead they pulled on Maskamal's tail.

"One, two, three, heave," cried Lima Bear. "One, two, three, heave."

They pulled and pulled, but the ship didn't budge. "This isn't working," Whistle-Toe said. "It's too big for us."

"One more try," Lima Bear said, tugging on Maskamal's tail. "One, two, three, heave!"

They pulled with all their might, and this time the rope started moving. "It's coming, it's coming," Lima Bear shouted. Inch by inch they pulled the rope in, their arms aching, until at last a large object came up. It was a big piece of the timber they had tied the rope to. The timber was so rotten that a piece had broken off.

"It's no use," Whistle-Toe said. "We can never pull up the ship. And besides, look how rotten it is."

"Fresna and I will go down one more time," Lima Bear said. "Just to look."

Once more, Fresna, Lima Bear and the on-and-off bugs dove into the bay. The ship hadn't moved at all. Fresna swam over to where they had fastened the rope. There was a new big hole in the side of the ship where the timber had been. Not only had the timber come loose, but several others had broken off and now lay on the ocean bottom.

Lima Bear peered into the hole, with all the on-and-off bugs going 'on' together. He saw a small chest inside and tapped excitedly on the inside of the mask; Fresna, understanding, tied the rope around the chest.

This time they all pulled with great excitement and soon the chest was out of the water and on the ledge. Whistle-Toe opened it. It was filled with gold coins, solid gold coins! They had found their treasure after all.

Now it wasn't a big chest, and there weren't that many gold coins inside, but there were enough to make them all feel very, very rich. They divided the coins up evenly because each had done something.

Whistle-Toe had started the fund-raiser, Fresna had contributed most of the money and had done the diving, L. Joe Bean had fooled the scoundrels and saved their money, and, of course, Lima Bear had found the map in the first place and had insisted on trying to pull up the sunken ship. And as for Maskamal, well, they all forgave him, because without Maskamal they never would have found the Yola-reena.

Oh, and they all chipped in and gave the on-and-off bugs one coin.

They each felt rich for a long time afterwards. That is, everyone except Maskamal. He quickly spent his money on things he didn't need, and he soon had none left. He did, however, pay Whistle-Toe back the 40 cents he owed him before he spent it all.

They explored the sunken ship many more times to see if there was more treasure, but they never found anything else.

As for Trickman and Sly, they sailed off in search of the four treasures using a map that no one could ever tell which way was right side up. The map led them to the part of the ocean where big typhoons roared. One of the typhoons wrecked their ship, and it was a long, long time before they ever returned.

How Back-Back Got His Name

Can you imagine what it would be like to lose your back!!?
Well, that is exactly what happens to Plumton, the Opossum.
Lima Bear and his clever friends become detectives
searching for his missing back. Follow them as they try new
and different ways of thinking to solve the mystery.
See how they band together to protect each other
in times of danger! Will they ever find Plumpton's back?
Follow the story to find the answer.

$15.95

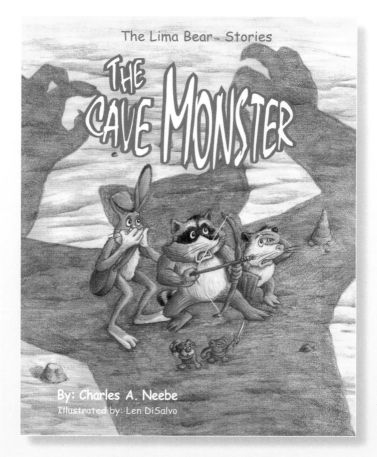

The Cave Monster

Oh, no!!! Sir L. Joe Bean, Lima Bear's cousin, has been captured by the Cave Monster. The Cave Monster is going to cook Sir L. Joe Bean and eat him. Lima Bear and his friends enter the dangerous Black Cave to save Sir L. Joe Bean. The Cave Monster attacks. Will they save Sir L. Joe Bean in time? And will they save themselves? Read on to see how bravely they fight the Cave Monster.

$15.95